M000226560

Letterville
The town that God built.

Sarh Bard?: Love

Letterville
The town that God built.

AARON SAIN

PUNCTUMEDIA
punctumedia.org

Letterville

© 2014 by Aaron Sain

All Rights Reserved.

All rights reserved. This book or any portion thereof may not be reproduced or used in any manner whatsoever without the express written permission of the publisher except for the use of brief quotations in a book review.

ISBN   978-0-692-28504-6
eISBN 978-0-692-28505-3

Punctum Media
102 White Cloud Trail
Murfreesboro, TN 37127
punctumedia.org

welcometoletterville.com

This book is dedicated to my parents, my sister, my wife, and my children. Never has a son, brother, husband, or dad, been so encouraged to chase after God's plan for his life.

**Of all the ways God could have described Himself...
He chose the alphabet.**

"I am the Alpha and the Omega..."
Revelation 1:8

CONTENTS

PROLOGUE

Only the Beginning

No rooster had crowed. The sun was not up. But no one was sleeping because the excitement was simply too much to take. The small town of Letterville had been waiting for this day for what seemed like forever. But it was finally here. Today was the day.

The brand new Alphabet Park was located in the middle of town-square. It was designed to be a quiet place where one could rest, take a leisurely stroll, or read a book - especially read a book - but not today. Today was the day when The Letters would be presented!

The park was alive with excitement as all of the townspeople anxiously filled the park looking for Him: The Creator of the Letters. The band began to play and everyone rose in anticipation and started to cheer. And then in a magical moment He appeared. The crowd became silent as all the letters filed in one by one and the freshly created letters were in awe as The Creator walked back and forth surveying his latest creations and then...He smiled.

"Welcome one and all," He said. "Today I am proud to introduce to you my newest creation, The Alphabet. I spent much time planning and crafting each of these letters and now they are ready to go into the world and achieve the purpose for which they were created."

He walked to the beginning of the line and carefully picked up the first letter.

"I needed a special letter to start the alphabet," He said, "and you are exactly what I was looking for. You shall be called the letter A." Everyone cheered and tried to get a good look as He displayed the letter A for all to see and then He gently set him back down and reached for the next letter. "You too are a special letter," said The Creator, "and you shall be called the letter B." Again everyone cheered, anxious to see what the next letter would be. "You are the letter C," He said.

And on and on it went until all twenty-six letters had received their names. The band played another song of celebration and everyone rushed to get a closer look at the letters and their Creator. The letters were busy getting acquainted with each other and trying to form words when The Creator noticed one letter all alone - not smiling. Not even a little. It was the letter U.

"Well, now what seems to be the matter?" The Creator whispered.

"I just don't think I'm special like all the other letters," U said. "I mean just look at some of them. Everybody's talking to A since he's the leader and all. And have you seen Z? How cool is that letter? K gets to start King and Q gets to start Queen. M looks like a majestic mountain and everybody's already figured out that E is going to be in way more words than any of the rest of us. And C? Now that's a special letter. Did you know it's the first letter in Creator?"

"Yes, I did know that," The Creator said. "And you're right, that is special. But so are you. I created every letter for a different purpose, and you are no less special than any of the other letters."

"But I'm the letter U", he said before he lowered his head and whispered, "I look like a bucket."

"I suppose you do look a little like a bucket," The Creator laughed, "but that will enable you to hold a great deal of my love. And that is going to come in handy. Why, you will be one of the most special letters in the alphabet. You see, the people who will use the alphabet will often get discouraged and when they need uplifting they will look to U. And when they need understanding again they'll need U. Why, I even chose U to begin one of my favorite words, unique."

U began to smile. "I guess I am special, huh?" he asked.

"As special as can be," said The Creator of the Letters. "Because you were created by me to be, well...U."

"What about me?" asked an excited E, for by this time all the letters had gathered to hear what The Creator was sharing with U.

"And me?" asked a quizzical Q.

Other letters were also curious and began to chime in, "Yes! What about us? Do you have plans for us, too?"

"Indeed I do!" answered The Creator. "I have plans for all of you and a future greater than your imagination!"

Then all the Letters began to rush forward shouting, "Tell us! Please tell us!"

The Creator smiled His biggest smile and laughed His heartiest laugh as He pulled all the letters near and said, "All in good time my creations, all in good time. For this is only the beginning!"

CHAPTER ONE
THE LETTER A
2 Corinthians 4:17-18, Philippians 2:1-8

It's Not Going to Stack Itself

A was not happy. Not even a little. And the worst part about it was he didn't know why. But The Creator did. He knew A was looking at things from a very sour point of view. So, The Creator took him for a walk.

"Would you like to learn a new word?" asked The Creator.

"Oh, yes! Very much!" said A, who was always eager to learn.

"OK then. Listen carefully," The Creator warned, "because this word is very powerful and has the ability to make one's life very magnificent or very miserable depending on how he uses it."

"There is a word that can do that?" asked A, who had never heard of such a word.

"Indeed there is," answered The Creator, "the word is attitude."

"An 'A' word! I like it already!" shouted A. "But what does it mean?" he asked.

"Well, A, most everyone has things to do they'd rather not do and places to go they'd rather not go. And everyone has things happen to themselves that they most certainly would not choose. But how one reacts to these things is what determines if one's attitude is good or bad."

"I'm not sure I understand." admitted A. "If something bad happens to me or if I have to do something I don't like, how can I possibly have a good attitude about it?"

"Let me tell you a story," answered The Creator.

"There once were two children whose parents were

very sick and bedridden. And because of this, the children had to do many chores that one would not expect a child to do. Each year before it was cold enough to snow, they had to cut and stack piles of firewood for the coming winter. And gathering enough firewood to burn from the first snowfall to the last is no easy task, no matter how one looks at it. Now, one child complained with every swing of his axe that gathering wood was not a child's job. He never ceased talking of all the fun he was missing and how unfair it was that none of his friends had to gather wood. Each afternoon, through their open bedroom window, his parents could hear him complaining, and that was a bad thing, for they loved their son very much and wanted him to be happy.

"The other child knew that the wood could not cut and stack itself and so he made a game of it and laughed and sang with every swing of his axe and smiled as the wood piles grew higher and higher. He also knew that when the snow began to pile up outside, all this work would help keep his ailing parents as warm as the freshly baked ginger cookies they would be enjoying inside by the fire. And that was a good thing for he loved his parents very much and wanted them to be happy."

Then, The Creator stopped His stroll and looked A in the eyes as He asked, "The children did equal chores and had the same number of swings of the axe, but which of the two boys would you rather be?"

"I want to be the one that sings and laughs!" shouted A.

"That's a great attitude! Then singing and laughing it shall be!" exclaimed The Creator.

And that is exactly what they did as they skipped hand in hand all the way back to Letterville.

CHAPTER TWO
THE LETTER B
Deuteronomy 31:6, Joshua 1:9, Proverbs 28:1

Hanging on by a Thread

B was still learning to read but she had no trouble reading the word "DANGER" posted above the old rope bridge that was strictly off limits to the citizens of Letterville. She knew better than to ever go near such a dangerous bridge but she continued to follow what she was sure were the cries of a small child. And sure enough, there in the middle of the bridge, hanging on to the thinnest piece of rope, was a small child in desperate need of rescue.

She wasn't exactly sure how far a voice would carry but B knew it wasn't far enough to reach the townspeople in the valley below, so she faced the fact that if this child was going to be rescued, she would have to do it. But B was scared and didn't want to help. However, B knew in her heart that not helping was not an option. And so she stepped onto the bridge.

B dared not look down as she slowly made her way across the failing bridge, testing each piece of rope before taking the next step. Her heart was pounding and her hands were as shaky as the old bridge when she finally reached the frightened child who was quickly losing his grip. With all her strength, B pulled the boy to safety and held him ever so tightly as they quickly retreated back to solid ground.

News of the rescue spread quickly and the next morning all the citizens of Letterville gathered in the square to celebrate and to present B with a Medal of Bravery.

"I am very proud of you B," said The Creator. "What you did was very brave indeed!"

"But I didn't feel brave at all" B whispered just before she was called to the stage, "I only felt scared."

"Well, of course!" laughed The Creator. "That was a very scary thing to do. But this Medal of Bravery has nothing to do with not being scared."

"It doesn't?" asked a confused B.

"Of course not. It has everything to do with what you did when you were scared. You see, B, the only difference between someone who is brave and someone who is not brave is the direction they go when they are scared. Only the brave head towards that of which they are afraid. And that is exactly what you did."

B smiled and asked, "Can I tell you a secret?"

"Always." answered The Creator.

"I'm scared right now! There are a lot of people in the crowd and they're all going to be looking at me."

"Then it is time to be brave again my friend," The Creator said encouragingly.

Just then the Mayor shouted, "Ladies and Gentlemen of Letterville, please make welcome today's hero and the bravest letter I know, the Letter B!"

As the crowd began to cheer, B once again faced her fear and made her way across the stage in front of all the citizens of Letterville. And to her surprise this time she even felt a little brave.

CHAPTER THREE
THE LETTER C
John 11:35, 1 Corinthians 13:1-13, Galatians 6:2, Colossians 3:12-13

Working Perfectly

"Come quick! Come quick! There's something wrong with C!" E shouted to The Creator. After all this was an emergency. Or so the letters thought.

When they came to where C was sitting, The Creator took one look at him and said, "Let me have a minute alone with my friend please."

As all the letters backed away, The Creator sat down next to C, put His arm around him and said, "Hello, C. Are you OK?"

"I don't know what's wrong with me," C said with his head hung low. "There is water coming out of my eyes and I feel funny inside." C paused and then whispered, "I'm afraid I might be broken."

"Well, I seriously doubt that," The Creator chuckled as He continued. "In fact, I think you are working quite well. Do you mind telling me what you were doing when this started?"

C wiped his eyes and began, "I was on my way to Market with a cart full of wonderful cakes and baked goodies when I saw a poor family sitting in the park sharing a very tiny portion of food. I saw them bow their heads and overheard them say your name and how thankful they were for what they had, but it was so little I knew they would still be hungry when it was all gone." C paused for a moment then said, "That's when I started feeling funny and water started leaking out of my eyes."

"I see," said The Creator, "and what did you do then?"

"I looked at my cart full of food and the tiny bit of food they had and decided that this simply would not do, so I rolled right up to them and offered them some of my most splendid pastries."

"Well that was a most kind thing to do, C. I am very proud of you and I'll bet it made you feel pretty good too, huh?" asked The Creator.

"Yes, sir. But when I walked away my eyes started leaking again and that's when the others came to tell you I was broken."

The Creator looked C straight in the eyes and said, "I want you to understand something very clearly. You are not broken."

"I'm not?" asked C.

"Not even a little," chuckled The Creator. "You are exactly as I intended…tears and all. You see you weren't leaking. You were crying."

"I guess I should be glad to learn a new 'C' word!" he said, "But 'cry' doesn't sound like a very happy word."

"Well, a lot of people will try to tell you that you shouldn't cry. They believe crying is a sign of weakness. But crying doesn't mean you are weak and not crying doesn't mean you are strong. Some people cry and some do not. But if one does cry, the real question is, what makes him cry?"

"I'm not sure I understand," admitted C.

"Let's say I had found you here today crying because you didn't get your way in some game you and your friends were playing. Well, that would be just silly wouldn't it?" asked The Creator.

"I suppose so," admitted C.

"I am proud of you C, not because you cried, but because you acted on what you felt inside. And that is called compassion."

"Another 'C' word! And a big one, too!" exclaimed C.

"And one of my favorites!" said The Creator. "You see, it's not enough just to feel sorry for someone. I am very proud of you because you showed compassion by sharing what you had with someone who needed it."

And with that C jumped up and grabbed his cart.

"Where are you off to in such a hurry?" The Creator asked curiously.

"There are a lot of people who need compassion," shouted C as he quickly pushed his cart towards home, "so I'm off to bake more goodies!"

And The Creator filled with pride as a line of letters followed C home to help with the baking. And to this day, if you visit the town of Letterville, the sweet aroma of cakes, pastries and compassion fills the air.

CHAPTER FOUR
THE LETTER D
Luke 6:31, Hebrews 10:24

It's Contagious

The citizens of Letterville have a very unique way of dealing with snow. Everyone is responsible for cleaning it from in front of his house or shop. No matter the task at hand, they firmly believe that if everyone does a little, no one has to do a lot. And that serves them well...most of the time.

The first flakes were tiny.

"Is it snowing?" asked Q.

"Technically, yes," answered T, "the water falling from the sky is now frozen, but I'd hardly call it snow."

"Well, I would. I love snow. The more the merrier," Q replied.

And then as if on cue, the flakes became larger and the amount became greater till there was no doubt...it was snowing...hard!

At first, only the grass and trees were white but then the sidewalks and roads became covered in millions and millions of little white visitors from the sky. All day long the snow fell until it was difficult to tell where roads ended and sidewalks began. Shops closed, everyone rushed home, and soon the city of Letterville looked more like a post card than a bustling city.

C and D arrived home at the same time.

"I'll see you in the morning, neighbor," D said as he rushed to the waiting warmth.

"Indeed. I'll see you in the street bright and early," replied C. And they both retreated indoors, safe from the winter blast.

When D awakened the next morning, he went to the

window to survey the task before him but all he could see was white. Everywhere. It had never snowed like this before and the town of Letterville was literally frozen in its tracks.

"I didn't know the sky could hold this much snow!" E exclaimed as she headed back inside.

"I don't think they make a shovel big enough for this!" shouted C.

Further up the block, H could be heard saying, "This is too heavy for me! No one could be expected to move this much snow."

And so the snow-buried streets were left undisturbed.

D pondered joining the others indoors and for a moment was tempted by the thought of a warm fire and a steaming mug of cocoa. But then he remembered all the people who would be counting on him to be in today. After all, people need a doctor when people need a doctor and germs don't stay home because of the snow. So, with snow shovel in hand, D braved the cold and headed out.

C was the first to hear the noise and looked outside. D was already through clearing a path in front of his house and was working on the road in front of E's house.

"Well, if D can do it, so can I," C said as he headed outside just in time to see E joining in the wintry battle.

F saw E and grabbed his shovel. G saw F and got busy as well. H decided if G could handle the weighty piles then she could too. And on and on it went till the streets were clear, shops were open, and patients were being made well.

At the end of the day, D had one more visitor to his

waiting room.

"Hello D," said The Creator.

"Hello! What brings you here on this cold winter's day?" asked D.

"I just want you to know that I am very proud of you. You helped a lot of people today."

"Yes, a lot of people seem to be sick these days," D replied.

"Oh, I'm glad you helped the sick, but that is not what I meant. You see, there's something else going around right now...and it's very contagious."

"Oh no. What is it?" asked a very concerned D.

"It's called dependability," He answered.

"Dependability?" D replied.

"Yes, but don't worry, it's a good thing!" said The Creator. "It means not letting people down when they're counting on you. And you are responsible for Letterville getting a very healthy dose of it this morning."

"Good," D said, "because I think I caught...ACHOO!... a cold."

"Well, don't you worry about a thing," said The Creator. "I'll take care of you if you get sick. You can depend on me!"

CHAPTER FIVE
THE LETTER E
1 Thessalonians 5:11, Hebrews 3:13

Faster, Higher, Farther

The town of Letterville is known for its magnificent festivals and celebrations and its citizens never miss a chance to throw a party. And today presented an opportunity if ever there was one. For today was the beginning of Letterville's biggest sporting event, The Games. Banners lined every street. Bands filled every stage. Special clothing and trinkets honoring The Games flew off the shelves of every shop. And everyone was on his way to The Games. Well, almost everyone.

"Hello E," said The Creator. "Quite the spectacle isn't it?"

"Too crowded if you ask me," grumbled E, "it really does make it hard to get home."

"Home?" The Creator asked, seemingly confused.

"Yes, home. I've been trying to get there for quite a while."

"You mean you're not participating in The Games?" asked The Creator.

"No sir, I'm not much of a runner," confessed E.

"Well, E, there's a lot more to The Games than running," hinted The Creator.

"I don't really jump either," said E, and guessing what The Creator would say next, added, "and I've never been good at throwing things either, so what's the point?"

The Creator smiled and said, "The point is there's more to The Games than what takes place on the field and I'd like to show you. E, I would like for you to be my helper at The Games. Would you like that?"

"Me? Help you?" exclaimed E. "I'd like that very

much! Let's go!"

As the first race of the day began, E was still wondering how she was going to help The Creator when she looked down from the stands onto the field and suddenly shouted, "There's my friend Q! She's the quickest runner I know! Why, I'll bet she's the quickest runner in all of Letterville!"

But Q wasn't doing so well. In fact, she was in last place.

"I wonder what's wrong with your friend today," said The Creator.

"I'm not sure. Maybe she's not feeling well," answered E.

"Or maybe she's sad that you're not here."

"But I am here," argued E.

"True. But does she know that?" asked The Creator pretending to not know the answer.

There was only one lap to go when E remembered telling Q that she would be very busy and wouldn't be at today's race.

"Do you think that's why she's behind?" asked E.

"There's one way to find out," answered The Creator.

So, with her loudest yell, E shouted, "Go Q! Go! You can do it!"

And what a yell it must have been because Q looked up into the stands and saw E yelling for her to hurry. And that is exactly what she did!

"And the winner is...Q!" shouted the announcer over the crowd celebrating the amazing come-from-behind victory.

The Creator smiled as He looked at E and said, "Thank you for helping me today."

"But I don't know what I did," E admitted.

"Q needed encouragement and I needed you to make that happen."

"An 'E' word!" said E, who was always eager to learn a new word. "What does it mean?"

"Well, it's very simple, E. It didn't matter that I and everyone else in Letterville believed that Q was the fastest runner. It might not have even mattered if Q believed it. What she needed to hear was that you, her friend, believed it. Sometimes people just need to hear that someone believes in them. Q heard you cheering her on and that is called encouragement."

"Wow! I guess there really is more to The Games than running, jumping and throwing," E said.

"Indeed. A lot more!" The Creator laughed as He turned his attention to the next event.

And for the rest of the day E never stopped cheering. And the runners ran faster...the jumpers jumped higher... and the throwers threw farther.

And The Creator's smile grew wider and wider.

CHAPTER SIX
THE LETTER F
Ephesians 4:32, Colossians 3:12-13

Back to the Attic

The citizens of Letterville are a happy bunch! But The Creator had been watching F for quite a while and noticed that he wasn't quite himself anymore. And though he was responsible for the word 'fun' (one of the most popular words amongst the town-folk of Letterville), lately F was having none of that. The Creator knew why and, as He often does, decided it was time for an experiment.

"You wanted to see me, sir?" F said timidly as he walked into The Creator's workshop.

"Well, hello F!" said The Creator as He rose from His bench to greet His most welcome guest, for the door to The Creator is always open to everyone. "Yes, I wanted to see you very much. I want to know if you will help me with something."

"Me? But of course!" exclaimed F.

The Creator looked F in the eyes and said, "I must warn you that while this will not be easy, I would never ask you to do something that would be anything but good for you."

"You promise?" asked a nervous F.

"Indeed," answered The Creator.

"Then I'll do it!"

"Great," said The Creator. "Wait right here, please."

After excusing Himself to the attic, The Creator returned with a large wooden trunk around which was wrapped a very heavy chain.

"Do you want me to help you open the trunk?" asked a curious F.

"Oh, no. Quite the opposite," answered The Creator. "I don't want you to open the trunk at all. I simply want you to take the trunk with you. In fact, for one week, I want you to take it with you everywhere you go."

F looked at the size of the trunk and said, "But it's so big, it must be very heavy."

The Creator smiled and said, "Oh, I think you'll manage just fine. But there's one more thing you must promise for this experiment to work."

"Anything," F stated firmly.

"You must hold on to the chain until you return here in one week. You can never let go of it – not even a little. The trunk must always be with you. Agreed?" asked The Creator.

F reached for the chain and said, "That sounds awfully hard but a promise is a promise. I'll do it!"

And with that, F dragged the trunk out the door and headed home, which was going to take a while, for indeed the trunk was very heavy.

One week later, The Creator stood and watched as F struggled to drag the trunk down the road towards the workshop.

"At last!" said an exhausted F as The Creator helped him drag the trunk the final few feet.

Already knowing the answer, The Creator asked, "How was it, F?"

"It was awful. No matter what I tried to do, the trunk was there," said a very frustrated F. "It's all I could think about!"

"Well, congratulations just the same," said The Creator, "but don't let go of the chain just yet. I have one more thing I need you to do." The Creator paused then said, "I want you to open the trunk."

F slowly released the latch, opened the lid, and stood speechless. For inside the trunk was a single piece of paper with the name of a friend who had hurt F's feelings a very long, long time ago.

The Creator looked F in the eyes and softly said, "I know you were hurt by your friend and for that I am very sorry. But F, you have hurt yourself more by not moving past the hurt and getting on with the business of living. You have carried around the hurt just like you have carried around this trunk all week. It was always with you and it kept you from being what I need you to be. It's time to forgive."

"But I can't just forget what my friend did," F said firmly.

"And I don't expect you to," said The Creator. "You see, F, forgiveness has very little to do with forgetting and more to do with letting go. Do you think your friend was bothered at all this week because you carried around this trunk?"

"No, sir. Not at all," answered F.

The Creator smiled and said, "Forgiveness is for you. Not them."

F stood frozen for a moment and then softly said, "I think I'm ready to let go of the chain now."

The Creator nodded in agreement.

As the chain hit the floor The Creator put His arms around F and asked, "Do you feel better?"

"I feel like my old self...only better!" shouted F. "Now can you help me with something?"

The Creator laughed and said, "Anything!"

"Great! Help me put this trunk back in the attic, please. I don't think I'll be needing it anymore!"

And together they moved the trunk one last time.

CHAPTER SEVEN
THE LETTER G
Proverbs 19:17, Hebrews 13:16, 1 John 3:17

Bless You

G suddenly felt weird inside. And although he wasn't exactly sure why, it was a good weird.

G had toys...lots of toys. He had so many toys in fact that he had forgotten what it was like trying to fit all of them into a toy box and was now worried about how to keep them from spilling out of a very full toy closet.

"You can have that if you want it," G said to P. And that's when he began to feel weird inside.

"For real?" asked P who wasn't used to having such amazing toys. "Thanks! I really wanted one of these for my birthday but I didn't tell my parents."

"Why in the world wouldn't you tell them what you wanted?" asked a very confused G. "I'm sure they'd love to get you what you want."

"Oh, I know they would love to," P explained, "but wanting to and being able to are two very different things."

G used to spend a lot of time with P's parents when they lived just a few doors down and thought them to be some of the finest folks he had ever known. But when P's dad got sick, they moved to a different part of town, sold a lot of their stuff, and P even had to change schools. Remembering this, G suddenly felt funny again. But this time it wasn't a good thing. G had so many toys that he had forgotten what it was like to want but not have.

"I've got to go," said P. "It's going to be dark soon."

"Have fun with your new toy!"

"I will! And thanks again!" P shouted as he sprinted towards home.

The next morning before breakfast, G was out the door with a bag of toys so large it was a wonder he could even drag it.

"Where are you off to so early?" asked his mom.

"I'm going to have fun with my toys!" replied G.

And fun it was! In fact, that day he had the most fun he'd ever had with toys. The sun began to lower in the sky, and as G was making his way home, he ran into someone he loved very much.

"Hello, G!" said The Creator. "What are you doing?"

"I'm having fun with my toys!" answered a very tired G.

"What toys? All I see is an empty bag."

"Oh. I guess it is empty now," said G. "Nice!"

"Nice?" asked The Creator. "Why is it nice that all your toys are gone?"

"I don't know exactly," said G. "All I know is, this morning the bag of toys was full but my heart felt empty. But now the bag is empty and my heart feels full."

"Well, I do know why," said The Creator. "Because I made you that way! That's what giving does to you."

"Giving?" asked G. "That's a G word!"

"And one of the most important, too!" said The Creator. "You see G, I am very capable of blessing those in need if you never give. But when you do, I get to bless you as well! Without giving, the world would be a very sad place…"

"...for everyone," G said.

"For everyone indeed," chuckled The Creator.

G spent the rest of his day playing with his new friends enjoying their new toys.

And The Creator spent the rest of His day blessing them all.

CHAPTER EIGHT
THE LETTER H
Psalm 37:7, Psalm 46:10, Jeremiah 2:25 (The Message)

Better Eggs

In the weeks following their unveiling, the letters did a wonderful job discovering new words, learning what they meant, and putting them into practice. But H seemed a bit too attached to one word so The Creator decided to pay her a visit.

"Hello, H," said The Creator.

"Oh, Hello!" replied H. "I didn't see you there."

"Yes, I noticed you were rushing right along. In fact, I've noticed that quite a bit lately."

"Why, thank you, sir," said a very proud H. "Did you know I have shaved 20 minutes off my morning routine? And I now get to work and back in the time it used to take me just to get to work. I've become quite the time expert."

"But at what expense?" asked The Creator.

"I'm not sure what you mean," answered a confused H.

The Creator smiled and said, "Would you like to conduct an experiment?"

"Very much," said H, "anything to help you!"

"Well, I think this will help you more than me but let me explain."

The next morning H hopped out of bed and began to speed through her morning routine but paused when she remembered what The Creator had asked her to do. So, she actually sat down to eat breakfast and had the best eggs she'd had in weeks. She walked to work, which was considerably slower than what she was used to but somehow she felt more alive in the morning air. She couldn't remember the last time she'd taken that long for lunch and found the conversation even better than the food. On the way home, she noticed her elderly neighbor Ms. Adams struggling to carry her groceries and lent her a hand. And then to top the day off, she simply sat with her and talked a while. Later that evening, she gave thanks for what she believed was the best day she'd ever had.

The next morning as H walked to work she saw The Creator ahead and shouted, "Good morning!"

"Oh, hello, H. How did the experiment go yesterday?"

"Excellent!" answered H. "In fact, I'm doing it again today."

"Glad to hear it!" said The Creator, "I believe you were the victim of an H word."

"An H word?" asked H.

"Yes. The word is hurry and you were really good at it," The Creator chuckled. "Too good if you ask me."

H was quiet for a moment then said, "But I thought hurry was a good word. Couldn't I do more if I hurried?"

"I suppose you could do more, but life is not about more, it's about better. And yes, hurry is a wonderful word sometimes. Firemen use it to put out fires. Athletes use it to win competitions. It has all kinds of delightful uses. But let me ask you a question. How was breakfast yesterday morning?"

"It was wonderful! Best eggs I've ever had."

"Were they different eggs?" asked The Creator.

"No. Come to think of it, they were same eggs I always

have but yet they were better. Why is that?"

"Easy. Because you took the time to enjoy them," said The Creator, "and I suspect eggs aren't the only thing you enjoyed yesterday."

"Indeed! Yesterday was simply the best," said H. "I saw all kinds of things I've been missing and enjoyed so much I had forgotten about. Including talking with you."

"Great! Isn't slowing down wonderful?" asked The Creator.

"Yes, but if you don't mind, I do need to hurry along this morning. I am having breakfast with Ms. Adams. We're having eggs!"

As H sped away, The Creator laughed and said, "Now that is a good reason to hurry!"

CHAPTER NINE
THE LETTER I
Genesis 1:27, Psalm 139:13-14, 1 Samuel 16:7, 1 Peter 3:3-4

A Handwritten Letter

Dear I,

My hope is that you keep this letter with you always. Read it often. I will remind you. I hope you always love yourself the way I do but...

There is a lot of power in the word I and you will be tempted to put too much emphasis on it from time to time. The temptation to love yourself more than you ought may be overwhelming at times. Some will tell you that your happiness is all that matters – that what you want is worth getting at all cost. They will tell you that happiness is found within you not me. They are wrong.

Others will tell you that you have no worth. But you have eternal worth because I created you and your value should never be determined by anyone other than me. And while loving yourself too much is dangerous, not loving yourself enough is equally damaging. I want you to feel good inside and out. But I want you to base those feelings only on one thing; you are made in my image and no one else's. When others tell you what they think about you remember, only my opinion matters.

Believe in yourself, but put your faith in me.

Trust in your own abilities, but rely on my strength.

Listen to your heart, but follow my direction.

Love yourself, but love me more.

And if by chance you ever find yourself doubting my love, and therefore failing to love yourself the way you should, close your eyes and repeat after me:

I am not an accident of nature.

I am meant for more than chance and happenstance.

I am more than skin and bones here on this planet.

I am a soul that loves to sing and dance.

I am made.

I am planned.

I am loved...by I AM.

Forever yours,
The Creator

CHAPTER TEN
THE LETTER J
Psalm 68:3, Luke 6:22-23, Galatians 5:22, John 15:11,

Free for All

C was confused, W wondered what it could be, and M was just plain mad. And as much as E hated to admit it, she and all the other letters were envious.

Everyone agreed. Something was definitely up with the letter J and they were determined to get to the bottom of it.

Word soon reached The Creator that the letters were talking about J and He promptly called a meeting.

"Hello everyone. I'll get right to the point. It has been brought to my attention that you all are jealous of J," said The Creator, "and I would like to ask you all just exactly why you are jealous."

K was the first to raise her hand, "That's just it. We don't know," she said.

"But there is something not right and we want to know what it is!" inserted D.

N stood up and said, "She seems too happy. It's just not normal."

"She obviously has something! Why else would she be so happy all the time?" asked E.

"Is it money?" M shouted from the back.

"She's quite popular. I'll bet that's it!" said P.

"Actually, it's none of that." said The Creator as He motioned for J to step to the front.

The letters truly did love each other and felt bad as J made her way forward. The room grew quiet as The Creator reached out His arms to embrace J and softly said, "J has something alright. But it's nothing that any of you aren't capable of possessing as well. And the best part is, it's free and there is an unlimited supply that I would like to share with each of you."

"Oh! What is it?" asked Q.

"Yes, what is it? Please tell us!" said the curious letters.

"OK, OK. Quiet everyone. It's very simple," The Creator smiled and said. "You all assumed that some 'thing' was giving J an extraordinary amount of happiness, when things and happiness have nothing to do with it. She is not happier than any of you. She simply has joy."

"I don't understand," said M.

"Well, M, you wondered if J had a lot of money, and while there is nothing wrong with having a lot of money in itself, it doesn't determine one's joy. There are joyful rich people and there are joyful poor people. P, you thought J's popularity was the answer, but how well one is known has no bearing at all on one's joy. There are joyful popular people and there are joyful unpopular people. There are even joyful happy people and joyful sad people."

"The Creator is right," said T. "Just last week J was very sad, but even then she seemed different. It must have been joy!"

"That makes sense," said M, "but how does one get joy?"

All the letters shouted together, "Yes, please tell us!"

"I have a better idea," said The Creator. "J, why don't you tell them?"

"There's nothing magical about it. I just know Him," J said as she pointed to The Creator. "When I'm having the best day, He's right there beside me, and when I'm scared, I know He's watching over me. When I'm happy, He celebrates with me, and when I'm sad, He sits beside me and helps me cry. And that brings me joy."

The letters admitted they had never looked at things quite that way before and apologized to J.

"We're sorry we were jealous, J," they all said, "and we promise to never let that J word steal our joy again!"

"Now that is cause for celebration!" said The Creator. And He smiled His biggest smile as one by one He brought joy to all the letters...even the sad ones.

CHAPTER ELEVEN
THE LETTER K
Proverbs 11:17, 1 Corinthians 13:4, Galatians 5:22-23, Ephesians 4:32

Baby Steps

The Creator has a way of seeing the potential in people even when they don't. He also has a way of seeing what's missing in someone when they don't see that either. And He had been watching K for quite a while and knew that with a bit of nudging she would become something very special: something for which she was created. And so K was invited to spend the day with The Creator.

Rather than lecture K or come right out and say why she was there, The Creator decided to simply show her. So, all day long, whether they worked or whether they played, The Creator was considerate and nice to K and went out of His way to do good things for her. And K noticed.

"I like how you are," said K.

"How do you mean?" asked The Creator.

"Well, you make me feel good inside. You do things for me that make me happy...things that are meant only to make me smile."

"Well, it's my pleasure," said The Creator "and I'm glad you noticed. It is called being kind."

"Hey, that starts with K!"

"It's a wonderful word," said The Creator, "and the world sure could use more of it."

Then with her head held low, K softly said, "I wish I was kind like you."

"Great!" said The Creator. "I think you'll do very well with that."

"Wait. Perhaps you misheard me, sir," said K, "I said I wish I was kind, not that I am kind."

The Creator chuckled, "I heard very well what you said. But wanting to be kind is the first step one must take in order to become kind. You see, K, kind starts as more something you do, not as something you are. So, go do kind!"

And so K did. Every day from the time she arose to the time she went to bed, she looked for opportunities to be kind. She was kind to her family. She was kind to her friends. She was even kind to complete strangers. And it wasn't long before she didn't even have to try. It was as natural as breathing. And the citizens of Letterville noticed.

Whenever they met they would say, "I wish I was kind like you, K!"

To which she would always reply, "Great! I think you'll do very well with that."

And The Creator always agreed.

CHAPTER TWELVE
THE LETTER L
Psalm 119:105, Isaiah 30:21, John 8:47, John 10:27-28

Take a Hike

The Creator loves to spend time with His creations. But it had been a while since He and L had spent time together and that simply would not do. So, The Creator paid L a visit.

"Hello, L," said The Creator.

"Hello!" replied L.

"I haven't heard from you in a while and I was wondering if you would like to spend a day together."

L shouted, "Absolutely! A whole day?"

"How about a day of exploring?" asked The Creator.

"Sounds exciting!"

"Then be at the forest's edge tomorrow morning and exploring it shall be!"

L could hardly sleep that night for thinking of an entire day exploring with The Creator. At the first hint of light, L sprang from his bed, leapt out the door and didn't stop running till he reached the forest's edge. The sun was beginning its journey over the horizon when he arrived but there was no sign of The Creator. L had never known Him to be late for anything before and was beginning to worry when he noticed a note with an "L" on it attached to a large tree. He opened it...

Dear L,

I've been looking forward to this day together. Even though this may not be what you had in mind, I know you'll have a wonderful time exploring places you've never been. You have nothing to be afraid of if you follow the path I've made for you. I will be with you every step of the way, but if you get scared just talk to me. If you get lost...all you have to do is listen.

Trust me,

The Creator

At first, L was confused and disappointed but The Creator had never let him down before, and he knew this time would be no exception so off into the woods he went. He spent the morning walking along the path that led him to places he'd only dreamed about. He met the most interesting creatures and saw things he thought only existed in books and legends. He ran and played like never before, enjoying everything The Creator had made for him to enjoy till he was stopped dead in his tracks by a fear that he thought too only existed in books. He was lost!

He ran this way and that way but the path never appeared. He searched in every direction as far as his eyes could see, but all he found were trees. Just more and more trees. Yelling for help was pointless this deep in the woods, still he yelled his loudest yell. But no one heard, so no one came. So L did the only thing he knew to do, he sat down and began to cry. And that's when he remembered the note. He pulled it from his pocket and read The Creator's words again, "…if you get scared just talk to me. If you get lost… all you have to do is listen." And so he did.

As L emerged from the woods he heard his favorite voice, "So how was your day of exploration, L?" asked The Creator.

"Amazing! Only one thing could have made it better," answered L.

"Oh, what's that?"

"If you would've been with me."

The Creator put His arms around L and softly said, "But I was, L. I was with you every step of the way. I felt all the joy you did today! I watched you every step of the way, I heard you singing and laughing and L, I even heard you when you talked to me."

"I heard you, too!" said a proud L.

"I told you all you have to do is listen," The Creator laughed and said.

"And that's good to know because tomorrow I'm going exploring again! Will you be joining me?"

"Every step of the way," said The Creator, "every step of the way!"

CHAPTER THIRTEEN
THE LETTER M
Matthew 5:7, Luke 6:36, Romans 5:8, James 2:13

No Fair!

Letterville is a safe place to live. Most of its doors have never seen a lock, and keys are rarely needed for those that have. So, word spreads quickly when a trespass occurs and the seats of the seldom-used courtroom fill even quicker. The Creator was slowly beginning to let the letters handle their own matters, but He was anxious to see how they would handle this particular one, so He quietly slipped in the back as things began.

"I say we run him out of town!" shouted one.

"Let's throw him in jail!" yelled another.

Someone else cried out, "Make him pay ten times over!"

"Does anyone else have a proposal for dealing with this matter?" asked the judge.

Then from the back of the room a hand was raised and the letter M stood and said, "I'd like to take him home with me."

Immediately the courtroom erupted in confusion as people gasped at the very idea.

"Approach the bench," demanded the judge, "for surely I misheard you!"

"I'd like for him to stay with me if that's OK, sir," repeated M as he moved to the front of the room.

"Give me one reason why I would allow that? Bad people simply do not belong with good people."

"With all respect, sir, if he were bad, that is precisely where he'd belong, but I do not believe he is bad."

"Not bad?" the judge responded. "He was caught red-handed."

"True. But I believe people are neither good nor bad. They are simply people, who make good or bad choices."

"Maybe so, but the choice was made, so why do you want to do this?" asked the judge.

M was quiet for a moment then said, "Because someone did the same for me once."

And with that the room grew very quiet for everyone knew M to be only good and kind.

"I didn't deserve what I was given. For what I deserved was punishment, but what I received was love," M continued. "And I believe that we are all supposed to receive that which we do not deserve and I simply want to make sure that is what he gets."

"But what shall I write in the book as his sentence?" asked the judge. "For with that, justice would not be served."

Then from the back of the room came a most familiar voice.

"Let the record show that he received something greater than justice." And silence overtook the room as The Creator made His way to the front.

"I fear you all have forgotten that M is not the only one who has received that which he did not deserve. Justice for those in need is a most beautiful thing," He continued, "but when it comes to the offender, reach first for mercy. As I have done for you."

"He's right," confessed C. "I once made some very bad

choices but was shown mercy."

G added, "I was guilty as well but was given only love."

And all around the room, Letters admitted to never getting what they deserved but only that which they did not. And one by one, they asked the judge to grant M's request: for the desire to show mercy is at its strongest when remembering one has received mercy.

The courtroom became quiet again as the judge began to speak.

"Until today, this court has always tried to be fair. But being fair would demand punishment, so today I choose to be unfair," the judge said as he raised his gavel. "I choose mercy over justice! Case closed."

The courtroom burst into applause as the gavel slammed down and The Creator smiled His biggest smile watching the room fill with mercy as M embraced his new houseguest. And to this day, if you visit the town of Letterville, you will find it to be most unfair...just as The Creator intended.

CHAPTER FOURTEEN
THE LETTER N
Proverbs 16:9, Luke 14:28, Ephesians 5:15-17

Riddle Me This

Wanting to help everyone is a good thing. But trying to help everyone can keep you from doing that very thing. And N was trying very hard lately.

As the sun began to rise and the streets of Letterville began showing signs of life, The Creator greeted His creations as He went for a stroll through town.

"Hello, S," said The Creator.

"Hello. Have you seen N?" asked S. "She said she'd help me stack these supplies on the shelves but she's missing as a six-year-old's front tooth."

C chimed in, "She said she'd help me carry all these crepes to the corner market but left after only three carts. Can you tell her I really need her help since she promised and all?"

"Well, hello, C," answered The Creator. "I have not seen her today but yes, I will tell her when I do."

It seemed as though The Creator could not pass a shop without someone mentioning N's promise to help followed by an observation of her whereabouts. But as He always does, The Creator knew just what was going on and set out to find her. And sure enough, when He found her, N was indeed helping someone.

As The Creator drew close, He noticed that N looked exhausted and not at all happy.

"But we're only half-way through," said H, "and you said…"

"I'm sorry I can't stay and help you finish, " said a sincere N, "but I promised a lot of others I'd help them today and I really must be going."

And with that, N was off to the next commitment.

"Hello, N," said The Creator. "How is your day going?"

"Awful. I'm trying very hard to please everyone but I only seem to let them all down."

"I'm sorry to hear that," said The Creator. "I know you're in a hurry but I think you should take a break. I have something I want to share with you."

"With me?" asked a curious N who was very happy to be sitting for a moment.

"Do you like riddles?" asked The Creator.

"I love them!" answered N. "Let me have it!"

The Creator smiled and began, "There once were two men. The first man rarely said yes to calls for help, but often helped many. The second man often said yes to calls for help but rarely helped any. How can this be?"

"I said I love riddles, but I didn't say I was good at solving them," N said as he scratched his head searching for an answer.

"Well, maybe this clue will help," said The Creator. "When you say yes to most things, you become bad at some. But when you say yes to less things, you become better at most."

After a few moments, N lowered her head and softly said, "I think I have it. I've gotten really good at saying yes, but really bad at doing it."

"Exactly, N," said The Creator. "The first man knew it

was impossible to always say yes, so he chose carefully what he would do, gave it his all, and his help was always worth having. The second man thought he could do it all and always said yes, but was stretched so thin and stayed so tired that his help was rarely worth having."

"Tired, huh?" asked N. "Sounds familiar."

The Creator put His arm around N and said, "No one can do it all, N...not even the good things. Your heart is so big that you want to help everyone and that is a good thing. But when one tries to help everyone, he often ends up helping no one."

"That sounds familiar, too," said N. "So what do I do?"

"Easy. To be good at helping people there is a word you must learn to use," said The Creator. "It is a very small word: simple to pronounce but difficult to say. And it starts with an N."

"Then I like it already! What is it?"

"The word is no and you must learn that it is a perfectly acceptable answer," said The Creator, "but examine your heart each time before using it for it seems that those who shouldn't use it do, and those who should don't."

N laughed and said, "Sounds like another riddle!"

"Indeed," chuckled The Creator. "Do you understand?"

"No." said N.

"You don't understand?" asked a bewildered Creator.

"Oh, yes! I was merely practicing," said N. "I understand. I'm not really helping if I'm not really helping, huh?"

The Creator said, "Well, I guess the only acceptable answer to that question would be, no!"

And they both laughed as they headed back into town to finish what they started.

CHAPTER FIFTEEN
THE LETTER O
Proverbs 17:22, Philippians 4:8, Romans 12:2

I Can See for Miles and Miles

O was headed to summer camp. And that was a good thing. But The Creator knew that N was filling O's head with some very negative thoughts. And that was a bad thing.

"It's that bad?" asked O.

"It's worse!" said N. "The people are the very opposite of nice and care only about themselves. It is a dreadful place full of boring days and miserable nights."

"Hello!" said The Creator, as He pretended to happen upon them.

As if rehearsed, N and O both answered together, "Oh, hello!"

"N, do you mind if I have a minute alone with O?" asked The Creator.

"Not at all," replied N, who hoped The Creator hadn't been listening but knew that He was.

"What's this I hear about you not wanting to go to camp?" asked The Creator.

"Well, I've heard awful things about it. It's a terrible place where fun is rarely welcome."

"But you've never been?" asked The Creator.

"No sir. If I had but one wish though, it would be to not go to that place."

"Well, I wouldn't want you to go to a camp to which you dreaded going," said The Creator, "but how would you like to go to one of my favorite places?"

O perked up and said, "Really? That would be great!

Please tell me about it."

"Well, for starters, the counselors there are most won-derful! They are kind, loving, devoted, and only care about making sure you have the most splendid time," said The Creator. "It sits atop Tall Mountain and its beauty simply cannot be matched. There's a porch overlooking an endless valley where some say you can see forever – and my cre-ations often gather there to spend time with me."

"You'll be there too?" asked an excited O. "When do I leave?"

A few days later, The Creator spotted O sitting on the porch quietly staring off into the distance.

"Hello, O," said The Creator. "How is your week going?"

"Well, it is nothing like you said it would be," O said, barely able to hold back his biggest smile. "It's better!"

The Creator laughed and said, "Well, I have a secret to tell you."

"A secret?" asked O.

"Indeed," said The Creator. "Remember that awful place your friend told you about?"

O answered, "How could I forget such a frightful place? I would never want to visit there."

"Well," said The Creator as He surveyed the beautiful valley, "you are there, O."

O looked at The Creator with his most confused look and said, "I don't understand. I thought it was a horrible place."

"Exactly. Before, you thought you were going to a very horrible place and if you had come here believing this to be that place, that is most certainly what you would have found," said The Creator. "But you came here believing the people were good and kind; therefore that is what you found. You saw beauty everywhere. And you also believed that you would find me here, so here I am," said The Creator.

"And I'm very glad you are here," said O.

"As am I," The Creator replied. "There is an old saying you would do well to learn, O, 'Things are as one thinks they are.'"

"I like that saying," said O.

"And there's a word for thinking that things will be splendid."

"Is it an O word?"

"But of course!" answered The Creator. "The word is optimistic."

"That's a big word!"

"And powerful, too," said The Creator.

O laughed and said, "You're telling me! It turned a dreadful place into someplace very enchanting!"

The Creator's laughter echoed through the valley below as O moved next to The Creator, looked far off into the distance and said, "I've heard that from this very spot, if you look hard enough, you can see forever."

"Oh? Well, what do you think?"

"I'm optimistic that I can!" said O.

The Creator put His arm around O and said, "Then I think you can too!"

And O spent the rest of the evening just sitting on the porch next to The Creator believing he could. Believing things to be splendid. And so they were.

CHAPTER SIXTEEN
THE LETTER P
Psalm 145:5, Ecclesiastes 3:11, Colossians 3:23,

Stop, Look, Listen

Autumn in Letterville is something to see! Golden leaves pile up like orange and yellow snowflakes and require about as much work to clean up as a deep winter snow. So, the neighborhoods were alive with the laughter of people wielding rakes and wheelbarrows in a never-ending battle against the descending adversary.

City clubs made quick work of cleaning the town square. Parents cleaned the grounds around the school. And groups of teens slowly made the rounds to elderly people's homes, taking a bit longer than necessary because everyone knows it's just about impossible to not jump in a fresh pile of leaves. It seemed as though the entire population of Letterville was in on the effort…everyone except the Letter P.

P was sitting all alone on his front porch with quite the frown on his face when The Creator spotted him.

"Hello, P," He said. "What a wonderful day!"

"Wonderful? Hardly the word I'd choose," P shot back.

"The air is crisp. The sun is bright. What's not to love?" The Creator asked.

"In case you haven't noticed, there are a billion leaves in my yard. And I raked it just yesterday," P sighed.

"I'm sure you'll manage," said The Creator, trying to lift P's spirit.

"It just seems like a lot of work for nothing."

"Nothing? Just look at how beautiful the leaves are! I wouldn't say it's for nothing. P, would you do me a favor?"

The letters loved any chance to help The Creator so P

answered, "Of course. Anything."

The Creator said, "I want you to close your eyes."

"But you just asked me to look at all the leaves." P replied.

"I know, but now I want you to close your eyes and tell me what you hear. Listen closely."

"I hear people."

"Exactly. Do they sound unhappy?" asked The Creator.

"No, sir. They're whistling and laughing."

"But they're raking leaves which according to you is a worthless endeavor. So, why do you think they're happy?"

"I don't know. I guess they like raking leaves."

"Perhaps. But I think something else is going on and it starts with the letter P."

"It does? I love P words! Please tell me what it is."

The Creator put His arm around P and said, "The reason they are having fun and you are not is because of perspective."

"Perspective? That's a big word," said P.

"And a very important one, too. It has to do with the way one looks at things. For example, you see autumn as a time of a lot of meaningless work. They see it as a chance to be together and enjoy my beautiful creation! Same leaves. Same work. Different perspective."

"Wow. That is an important word!" said P.

"Indeed!" said The Creator. "Now that you know about perspective, I want you to open your eyes and tell me what you see."

P opened his eyes, smiled his biggest smile and said, "I see millions of beautiful leaves! I see people laughing and playing and enjoying their work! I also see something else."

"Oh, what's that?" asked The Creator.

"An opportunity! All these leaves mean I have a chance to make someone's day! I'm going to find someone who needs my help and I'm going to rake their leaves for them!"

"But what about the leaves in your own yard?" asked The Creator.

"Oh, they'll be here when I get back. And besides, there will be even more to jump in then!"

P was whistling as he grabbed his rake and headed to his neighbor's yard and The Creator laughed and said, "Now that is a good perspective!"

CHAPTER SEVENTEEN
THE LETTER Q
Psalm 23, Psalm 46:10, Isaiah 55:3, Jeremiah 33:3,
Lamentations 3:22-23

Deafening Silence

The Creator craves conversation with His creations. He loves hearing from them as much when things are good as when they are not. But lately Q's very good life was very busy and not only was she not talking to Him...she wasn't listening either.

"Have you heard from The Creator lately?" asked A.

"Why yes, just this morning," answered L.

"Me, too," said P, "and last night as well."

C spoke up, "We had the best conversation just a few minutes ago! What about you, Q?"

"Me? Uh. No, not lately. Busy, busy, busy, you know," Q answered.

And with that, Q hurried on her way.

The truth was that Q really wanted His help with something and had wondered why she hadn't heard from Him lately. The Creator was well aware that Q needed to hear from Him (but not for reasons she thought important) and He had in fact been trying to talk to her all day. He spoke through the beauty of the sunrise but she looked right past. He spoke through the music that she listened to as she went for her daily jog but all she heard was music. He tried speaking through a friend but she missed Him there as well. After work, she went to see some of A's beautiful art on display and failed to see what He was saying on each canvas, and she even missed it on the way home in the sunset painted on the evening sky. So The Creator did what He knew He had to do.

The first clap of thunder was as loud as any Q had ever heard. It had been quite a while since she had been through a storm like this and had forgotten how scary they could be.

"Surely this will pass in a short while," she thought to herself.

But it did not. On and on it raged getting ever stronger and ever more frightening.

"If only I could talk to The Creator, He'd know what to do. But He'll never hear me in this storm," she said.

Then in an instant a bolt of lightning brought total darkness to her house and she sat frozen, scared to move in the silence.

"Hello, Q," came a voice out of the blackness.

"It's you!" answered Q. "Where have you been? I'm scared."

"I know you are," answered The Creator, "and I've been trying to speak to you all day."

"You have? But I never heard you."

"I'm very aware," said The Creator, "but I've been speaking to you since before you awoke this morning. In fact, I've been trying to talk with you every day since we last spoke."

"It has been a while, hasn't it?"

"Indeed."

"Did you send the storm to get my attention?"

"Not exactly," said The Creator, "but I did send the quiet. Because I knew there you would hear me."

"I'm glad you did. I miss our talks," Q softly said.

The Creator put His arms around her and said, "I've missed you, too, Q. And I want you to know that no matter how busy you get, I am never too busy for you and I will always be waiting in the quiet."

Then as quickly as they died, the lights in her house came back to life.

The Creator smiled and said, "Well, I guess you won't be needing me tonight after all."

"Actually, could you stay for awhile?" Q asked.

"But don't you need to get ready for your busy day tomorrow?" asked The Creator.

"Yes. And that is exactly why I need you to stay."

And so He did.

Early the next morning as Q headed out for a jog, she saw Him in the morning sky and heard Him in the songs as she ran. She heard Him when she talked with friends and saw His beauty everywhere she looked. In fact, in time she found that she could hear Him just about anywhere, even in the noisy places...but always in the quiet.

CHAPTER EIGHTEEN
THE LETTER R
Proverbs 3:5-6, 2 Corinthians 7:10, Philippians 3:13, James 1:5

First Things First

There are certain words that make The Creator very happy. And then there are certain words that make Him very sad. And R was close to becoming very familiar with one of the latter. So, The Creator went to see her.

"Mind if I have a word with you, R?" asked The Creator.

"Well, Hello! Can you have a word with me? You can have as many as you'd like!" answered R, who always enjoyed time with The Creator.

"Let's sit down over here," said The Creator.

"Sounds serious," replied R.

"It is indeed. I need to tell you about an 'R' word but I'm afraid you might not like this one very much."

"But if it's not a good word, why do I need to know about it?" asked R.

"Because I love you," said The Creator, "and I'd rather share it with you now myself, than have you learn it the hard way on your own."

"Have I done something wrong?" asked a very concerned R.

"No. But I not only want to keep you from doing wrong things, I also want to help you do right things."

"I'm not sure I understand," said R.

"You know what choices are, right?" asked The Creator.

"Indeed. C told me all about them."

"Good. I'm glad he did because the word I need to share with you is about what happens after choices are made, specifically the bad ones. Have you ever done something that you later wished you hadn't?" asked The Creator.

"Yes, sir."

"Have you ever not done something that you later wished you had?"

R answered the same.

"Do you remember how you felt each time?"

R shook her head slowly and said, "I felt awful. I wanted to go back and do it all over but I couldn't."

"Well, that is called regret."

"You're right. I don't like that word very much," said R.

"Then the best thing you can do is try to never use it," said The Creator.

"But how do I do that?" asked R. "I always think I'm making a good choice. But later sometimes I realize I've made a bad choice." R paused a moment then continued, "You should know, I talk to you every time after I do that."

"Well," said The Creator as He put His arm around R, "what if you talked to me about your choices before you make them?"

"That would be splendid. You always make the best choices!" replied R.

"And I would like nothing more than to help you with yours."

R chuckled and said, "Good! Cause I could use the help!"

"Well, I didn't mean to hold you up. Weren't you on your way to do something?" asked The Creator.

"Yes, but I think I need to talk to you about it first," answered R.

The Creator laughed and said, "Now that's a good choice!"

And to this day, R always talks to Him before every decision. And that's something she never regrets.

CHAPTER NINETEEN
THE LETTER S
Matthew 25:35-40, James 4:17, 1 John 3:17

Who Me?

Finding people to offer unsolicited suggestions on things that need to be done is easy. Finding people to actually do them is not.

"There sure is a lot of trash in the street," S said as he entered his favorite pastry shop.

"It happens every time there's a storm," C agreed.

"Well, it's awful," he said. "Someone should do something about it."

"Enjoy your treats!" said C as S collected his goodies and headed to the door.

When S reached the sidewalk, he glanced across the street and paused to say, "Would you look at the weeds and tall grass in the cemetery? What an eyesore for anyone visiting our fair city. Someone should do something about that!"

S continued on his way and soon reached the park where children were playing. He couldn't help but notice that the swings were in need of repair, as were all the things on which children love to climb.

"Such a shame. What a wonderful place full of volunteers, yet the playground is in shambles. Someone really should do something about it," S complained.

He continued on his way but stopped when he saw some very poor people begging near the entrance to his neighborhood.

"I feel so badly for these poor people. What a shame they must beg just to get by. Someone really should do something about that."

Just then S heard a most familiar voice.

"Hello, S," said The Creator.

"Oh, hello!" replied S. "What brings you to my neck of the woods?"

"I was wondering if we could talk for a minute," said The Creator.

"But of course!" answered S. "What's on your mind?"

"Well, S, I've been listening to you today and I have good news for you."

"You do?"

"Indeed. All day long I've heard you complain that 'someone should do this' and 'someone should do that.' And I just wanted you to know that I know someone who can do all of those most worthy things."

"Oh, that's great! I've been wondering when someone would finally do something about it all. Who is it?"

The Creator put His arm around S and softly said, "It's you, S. You are someone."

"Me?"

"Yes, you," said The Creator. "S, no one is capable of doing everything. But everyone can do some things. And you are very capable of doing the things that you've seen today."

S looked at The Creator and said, "I guess I never thought of it like that before."

"Most people don't, S. But there is a lot of power in the word someone. Can you imagine what this world would be like if no one complained about someone not doing something but instead someone just did it?"

"I think it would be a most splendid place!" answered S.

"I think I agree!" said The Creator.

As S turned back towards town, The Creator said, "Where are you going? I thought you were going home."

"Oh, I was," S laughed and said as he stopped at the neighborhood entrance. "But I know someone who has an awful lot of things they need to do first!"

"And I know someone who makes me very proud," The Creator said, "very proud indeed."

CHAPTER TWENTY
THE LETTER T
Philippians 4:13, 1 Peter 5:7

That Was Easy!

It was the kind of day that makes one wish they had the power to stop time and leave everything frozen in that very moment. The sun was high and bright as ever and the few clouds that were in the sky were busy making the most splendid shapes for children's imaginations. The air was as crisp as the first bite of a freshly picked apple and the good citizens of Letterville were laughing, singing, and playing on every hill and in every valley as far as the eye could see. Today, everyone was enjoying the Creation. Well, almost everyone.

"Hello, T," said The Creator. "Why are your friends having to play without you?" He asked.

"I'm too embarrassed to say," T mumbled as she looked towards the river.

"There is no need to ever feel embarrassed with me. You can tell me anything," said The Creator.

T dropped her head and admitted bashfully, "I can't swim."

"You can't? Or you don't know how?" prodded The Creator.

"What's the difference?" T sighed with her head even lower than before.

"Why there's a big difference!" exclaimed The Creator. "Have you attempted to swim before and failed?"

"No, sir."

"Is someone preventing you from swimming?"

T wasn't exactly sure where The Creator was headed with these questions but again answered, "No, sir."

"Well, then this is easy! It's not that you can't; it's simply that you've never tried. And trying is easy!" stated The Creator. "Now, I can't promise that you will succeed upon first effort but I can promise you this – you will never swim if you never try. And that is something that I am simply not willing to accept." And so the two set out for the river.

To T's surprise, no one laughed when she told her friends she didn't know how to swim. In fact, E admitted that she herself had only recently learned to swim and that was very encouraging to T because she sank like a rock on her first try. But with the water not nearly deep enough to be over her head, she simply stood up and tried again. Then suddenly T felt very strange. She was moving through the water but could no longer feel the bottom. She was swimming!

Everyone cheered and splashed around in celebration of T's big achievement.

"One never knows what they are capable of until they try," said The Creator. "Just imagine all the good that people could do in this world if they would simply stop saying 'I can't do this' or 'I can't do that' and instead realized that what they should really be saying is, 'I've never tried.'"

"Yes, that really is a silly thing to say!" T shouted just before she made the biggest splash of the day. "After all, trying is easy!"

And The Creator smiled for now everyone was enjoying the Creation.

CHAPTER TWENTY-ONE
THE LETTER U
1 Thessalonians 5:11-14, Ephesians 4:29

Dry as a Bone

In the weeks and months following their unveiling, the letters became sadly aware that not every word they came up with was a good word. Some words simply described bad things but others were downright hurtful. And while he meant well, U was using more than his fair share of them lately.

"No, no, no," said U, "you're doing it all wrong. How many times do I have to tell you?"

"I'm sorry," said T who was adjusting to her life of attempting new things. "I will try to do better."

"Well, see that you do," U said as he made his way to the center of the floor. "Listen up people, we are supposed to be makers of umbrellas but lately all I see are makers of mistakes! Consider this a warning."

U didn't mean to come across hateful but productivity was at an all time low and with the approaching rainy season, the stress was almost more than he could handle. And as much as he loved keeping the citizens of Letterville dry, sometimes he wished he wasn't in charge. But he was, and he desperately needed to improve things in the shop or he was going to be all wet.

"Hello, U," said The Creator.

"O, hello. Sorry you had to see that," replied U. "None of the workers seem to be able to focus lately and leaky umbrellas don't make for very happy customers."

"I would think not. But I think I can help," said The Creator.

"That would be great! Maybe if you tell them what they're doing wrong they'll listen."

"I think they know very well what they're doing

wrong, U," said The Creator. "What I don't think they know is what they're doing right."

"But what they're doing right is very little," said a confused U.

"That may be true," said The Creator. "But I believe it's time for an experiment. Are you in?"

"I'm desperate. I'll try anything."

"Great. Then for one week I want to run the shop. You may observe but that is all. Agreed?"

"Like I said, I'm desperate. So yes, agreed," said a hesitant U.

So for the next week, U refrained from correcting a single mistake and only watched and listened as The Creator took over.

"Well, K, that may be the nicest batch of handles ever carved," The Creator said with a smile.

"Why, thank you sir, I am using a new knife. Maybe that's why," replied K.

The Creator laughed and said, "I don't believe the knife made the difference at all...you did! Keep up the good work!"

And that is exactly what K did.

"And as for you S, is that a new stitching process? I've never seen any quite so straight and watertight. Great job indeed. Keep up the good work!"

And that is exactly what S did.

In fact that is what every worker did.

Then U noticed something very odd. After a few days, The Creator no longer had to avoid mentioning mistakes for the only thing being made were the best umbrellas the shop had ever seen. In fact, they were selling more and better umbrellas than ever before. At the close of the week, The Creator said His days as shop manager were through and it was time for U to once again run the shop.

"I'm very confused," said U.

"I thought you might be," said The Creator. "Wondering where all the mistakes went?"

"A little. But what I'm really wondering is where all the smiles came from!"

"It's simple really," said The Creator. "People rarely need a reminder of that which they do wrong but instead need a reminder of that which they do right. So I choose to uplift."

"And that makes them happy!" U exclaimed, suddenly remembering what The Creator had told him the day of his unveiling.

"And better," answered The Creator. "You see, U, when one hears only of his mistakes, he soon begins to believe that is all he is capable of, and so that is what he does. But instead, if one hears of that which he is doing well, he soon believes that is what he is capable of and so that is what he does."

Just then the sky began to rain a most heavy rain and U fetched an umbrella for The Creator.

"Ah! I love the first rain of the season. Would you like

to walk with me, U?" asked The Creator.

"Thank you but I believe I'll stay here. I have some up-lifting to do!" answered U.

"Goodbye then," said The Creator as He made His way onto the sidewalk.

"Goodbye!" said U.

And as the rain poured down on the town of Letter-ville, The Creator walked and The Creator smiled. But He did not get wet.

CHAPTER TWENTY-TWO
THE LETTER V
James 1:27, Luke 10:25-37

Water, Water Everywhere

The rainy season was well underway and the citizens of Letterville were celebrating as they do each year, because a good time of rain means a bountiful Fall Harvest. But this year's rain was one for the record books and celebration soon turned to fear. So, as Mayor of Letterville, V called a town meeting.

"Citizens of Letterville. I have just returned from a tour of the dam and at the most we have one more day of rain before it breaks and our beloved town is flooded," she said as chaos erupted.

"What do we do?" shouted D.

"Where do we go?" yelled G.

T joined in, "How much time do we have?"

"Quiet everyone. I've asked The Creator to join us and He will answer all your questions," V said as she motioned to Him.

"We will begin evacuating immediately," The Creator said as He moved to the front of the room. "Return to your shops and neighborhoods, gather only that which is important, and proceed to higher ground." The Creator paused as He looked around the room and repeated, "Remember, gather only that which is important."

In a flash, the room emptied and everyone rushed into the streets that were beginning to fill with water.

"Leave no gold behind!" shouted one.

"Or silver!" said another.

"Our precious art can never be replaced! Don't overlook a single piece!" yelled another.

"Pack your cart carefully so you can save as much as possible!" the mayor shouted above the downpour. "Now, hurry!"

In no time at all, the exodus was underway and the rain-soaked streets were jammed with folks fleeing that which they hoped wouldn't come. Everyone moved quickly, carrying as many of their precious belongings as their cart would hold: furniture, fine china, toys, family heirlooms, musical instruments, as well as shop supplies and tools. And soon they arrived at higher ground where it was safe...all of it.

"Great job everyone! And none too soon! I've just received word that the dam is cracked and beginning to leak," proclaimed Mayor V, "but thanks to your efforts, we can rejoice that all that is precious to us is safe! I think we should spend some time thanking The Creator for taking care of us today!"

And so the citizens of Letterville sang and danced in the rain as they praised The Creator for their safety, and the valley below was filled not only with rain but also with the sound of celebration...but only for a moment.

"Look!" shouted L. "Down there!"

"It's The Creator!" said P.

"I see Him! But what's He doing?" asked Q.

L leaned forward to get a better look and said, "He seems to be looking for something."

"But what?" someone asked. "We got everything precious to us, did we not?"

Everyone watched in curiosity as The Creator searched

Letterville for whatever it was He was looking for. He looked here and He looked there. There was nowhere He did not look.

"Whatever it is, it must be important! I've never seen Him run like that before," said M. "We must have missed something very special. We have all the gold and silver, correct?"

"Indeed. And our shops and houses are empty. So, what could it be?" they all wondered aloud.

As The Creator stopped and knelt down to pick something up, the clouds overtook their view and everyone strained to see what was so important to Him that it would cause Him to search such a dangerous place. After disappearing from their sight for a few moments, they spotted Him making His way up the mountain, and a silence so quiet fell over the crowd that, other than the falling rain, all they could hear were tears hitting the ground. For in His arms were all the children whose parents had long since passed, as well as all the widows who now spent their days as the loneliest of Letterville's residents: all of whom had been forgotten by the onlookers.

No one spoke, but everyone moved down the mountain to help The Creator with His most precious cargo. When they had all safely reached higher ground, He broke the silence.

"My dearest creations, I very much want you to learn something today and the best way to do that may be by me teaching you a new word," He began. "When you place importance on something, it is called value. But you must understand that one cannot simply say that something is valuable to them for it to be so. Words can only claim that which one values, but actions prove that which one values. I know you think that I am disappointed in you for placing so much importance on the items in your carts that you overlooked these special creations I rescued," He continued, "but, while that does make me sad, it is not what broke my heart today. Today, you placed more importance on being with me than taking care of the ones you claim to love. You say that you only want to please me, but if you want to show true love for me, you will take care of these that you have forgotten. For that is what I value above all."

With that, V stepped to the front of the crowd and said, "Citizens of Letterville, this is a sad day indeed. For today, we have forgotten what it means to love and..."

"V! Wake up!" said L.

"It was a dream?" a startled V said as she sat straight up. "It was a dream!"

"Yes, V," said L, "You were talking in your sleep and you sounded very upset. Are you OK?"

"I am now that I know it was only dream," said V as she breathed a sigh of relief.

"Hey, good news!" L said. "While you were asleep it stopped raining and the repairs we made to the dam worked wonderfully! Our town is safe!"

As the workers made their way down to the town below, the citizens of Letterville lined the streets to thank them for saving their town.

"All we did was a bit of work on the dam," said the workers. "The Creator is the one who saved us! Let's spend some time thanking Him instead!"

And so they did. And The Creator smiled His biggest smile and felt very valued indeed, for in Letterville no child is ever without a family and no widow is ever alone.

CHAPTER TWENTY-THREE
THE LETTER W
Psalm 141:3, Proverbs 17:9, Proverbs 18:7, Ephesians 4:29

Sticks and Stones

Letterville is a happy place to live. The streets are filled with the sound of laughter more often than not. People pause and speak when passing and a simple, "How are you?" is more than a greeting; it is a genuine inquisition into one's state of being. Yes, in Letterville, conversation flows as it should between friends. But even the best of people can let their tongues get the best of them from time to time and the folks of Letterville are no exception.

"Did you hear?" asked one.

"I simply can't believe my ears!" said another. "Simply scandalous."

"I always suspected something like that."

"Well, let me tell you what I heard."

They meant well of course. Everyone knows that news this big isn't gossip and it simply must be talked about. So, in every shop, on every street corner, over breakfast, and over dinner, this is what consumed the citizens of Letterville.

W understood the virtue of thinking before you speak and remembered what The Creator had taught her about words, so it shocked no one more than her when she gathered all the air possible into her lungs and yelled in her loudest yell, "STOP!"

And just like that, everyone did.

"This is not right," she said. "Just listen. Do you hear one word that would help anyone? Do you hear one word that would make The Creator proud? Has anyone even talked to Him about this? Has a single one of us shown love or compassion or checked to see if it's even true?"

"She's right you know," said The Creator who had heard everything. And Letterville was as quiet as ever as everyone gathered to hear what He had to say.

"You have all been given the gift of words. But words are like hammers," said The Creator, "they can build up and they can tear down. Words have started and avoided wars, formed and ended friendships, strengthened and destroyed relationships, caused people to celebrate and cry, extended and denied hope, and they have given and taken life. Words are sometimes good and they are sometimes bad, but they are always powerful. Use them carefully for they can never be taken back."

"I think we need to use some words for good and go apologize," said A.

"I'll go!" said V.

"Me, too," said R. "I need to make things right."

C spoke up and said, "I need to see how I can help."

Then the Creator filled with pride as all the letters joined in to pick just the right thing to say. "Now those are some good words," He said, "and powerful, too."

CHAPTER TWENTY-FOUR
THE LETTER X
1 Corinthians 12

And the Oscar Goes to...

"Places everyone!" shouted the leader of the official Letter-ville Marching Band. "We've not a minute to spare. And One... Two...Three...Four..."

The annual Christmas concert was less than 24 hours away and preparations were at a fevered pace. The Creator was taking in all the hustle and bustle of the season and enjoying the final rehearsal when He noticed X lagging behind the band – obviously not in the holiday mood.

"Hello, X," said The Creator, "is something the matter?"

"Oh, I'm OK I guess. It's just hard to be excited when you're not needed."

"Not needed?" asked The Creator. "What makes you think you're not needed?"

"Well, my entire job is to push the xylophone, and honestly, if it didn't start with an X, I doubt I'd even be doing that. It's just hard not being important, that's all."

"Sounds to me like I need to let you in on a little secret. Would you like to hear it?"

"Of course I would!" answered X.

"I consider you to be one of the most important and hardest working letters in all the alphabet."

"You do?" asked X.

The Creator smiled at X and said, "I do indeed. I shudder to think what would become of this world without you."

"But I don't start any fancy or famous words at all.

How can I be important?" asked a confused X.

"Well, for starters, I think we need to define what important is," said The Creator. "You seem to think that only letters who start big words or get the spotlight are important. But I don't look at things quite the same."

"You don't?"

"Not at all. You see, most of the people think that only some of the people are important. But I happen to know that most of the people are wrong. Everyone is important," The Creator said.

"Everyone?" asked X.

"Everyone. Take you for example. You seem to think that being a helper is not important, but without you, X, Christmas presents would have no boxes. Broken toys could never be fixed. Doctors couldn't give exams, students couldn't excel, rooms would have no exits, grooms would have no tuxes, and no one could go the extra mile. Just think of all the things that could never exist without you, X. I'd say being a helper is pretty important, wouldn't you?" asked The Creator.

"Indeed!" X shouted as he ran to catch up with the band.

"Where are you going, X?" yelled The Creator.

"I have a most important job to do! This thing won't push itself you know."

Then songs of exaltation began to fill the air and The Creator smiled His biggest smile as He listened to every instrument in the band...especially the one that starts with X.

CHAPTER TWENTY-FIVE
THE LETTER Y
John 3:16, Romans 5:8, Romans 8:38-39, 1 John 4:16,

Look Harder

The sun was setting on Letterville and shops were closing for the day. And as He does at the end of everyday, The Creator made His way through town to check on His creations.

"Hello Y! I see you had a great day," said The Creator, "and I trust your night will be even better. I'll see you tomorrow."

"Oh, hello, sir!" said Y. "It was a good day indeed and I too hope to see you tomorrow. In fact, I was wondering if I could come see you for a change."

"But of course!" said The Creator. "Anytime. No invitation needed."

"Great. But can I ask you a question?" inquired Y.

The Creator laughed and said, "I believe you just did!"

"Well, I have another question then," replied Y. "Where do you live?"

"You know exactly where I live, Y," said The Creator, "we've met there many times."

Y replied, "I don't mean Letterville, sir. I need to know exactly where to go tomorrow if we're to spend the day together."

The Creator put His arm around Y and said, "Trust me, you'll know. And when you find it, we will visit indeed."

So the very next day, Y set out to find The Creator.

Y thought to herself, "The Creator is mighty and is loved by everyone. Surely He lives in a most fancy place!" And so she headed to the edge of town and knocked on the door of the biggest mansion in all of Letterville.

"Hello. Does The Creator live here?" she asked.

"The Creator does not live in this house," came the reply.

Then Y thought, "He loves the poorest among us and always shares what He has, therefore He must live in a modest dwelling." And so she made her way to the smallest shack in the poorest part of town.

"Does The Creator live here?" she asked.

"The Creator does not live in here," came the reply.

She searched high and she searched low. She looked near and she looked far. She travelled East and West and North and South but Y never did find what she was looking for.

Exhausted from a most tiring day, she returned home and prepared for a good night's sleep. And as she does every night, Y knelt beside her bed to talk to The Creator.

"Thank you for this day," she began. "I wanted to be with you but I still don't know where you live. You are so wonderful that I know it must be a magnificent place and I hope to find it tomorrow so we can spend the day together. Amen."

"Indeed I do live in a wonderful place," said The Creator.

Y opened her eyes expecting to see The Creator but only heard His voice.

"I looked everywhere for you today," said Y.

"Well, not exactly, Y," said The Creator. "There is one

place you have yet to search."

"There is? Where? For I looked in all of Letterville today."

Then The Creator softly said, "Have you looked in the mirror?"

Y turned to the mirror and was amazed that instead of her own reflection she saw that of The Creator instead.

"I don't understand," said Y.

"Well, Y, if I lived in a fancy dwelling then only he who lived there would be with me. And likewise if I lived in a shanty then only he who lived there would be with me. So not the greatest of mansions or the lowliest of shacks would ever do. I needed a place where we could always be together and never have to say goodbye, no matter where you dwell. So I live in you."

"A 'Y' word," Y humbly replied.

"And I want you to know that of all the words ever spoken, it is my favorite," said The Creator. "There is nothing I love more than you."

"So we can be together anytime?" asked Y.

"Anytime indeed," said The Creator. "For I am always with you. All you have to do is look inside."

Y smiled at that and said, "Then I must get to sleep because I would like to spend all of tomorrow with you."

"And I with you," said The Creator. "Goodnight, my friend."

Y could feel The Creator tuck her in and replied, "Goodnight, sir. I'll see you in the morning."

And The Creator smiled His biggest smile knowing that He would.

CHAPTER TWENTY-SIX
THE LETTER Z
Psalm 37:4-5, Romans 12:1-8

Making up for Lost Time

Z was ready for the opportunity to prove himself to The Creator as a worthy manager, but as foreman for the new Visitor's Center, he wasn't off to a very convincing start.

Normally, Z would be excited to see The Creator headed his way, but this project was giving new meaning to the phrase "behind schedule", so Z faked a smile and tried to disguise his half-hearted greeting.

"Hello."

"Well, Hello, Z. How's the construction coming along?" replied The Creator, pretending not to know the answer.

Realizing it was useless to pull one over on The Creator, Z offered up honestly, "It's just awful. We couldn't be anymore behind if we tried."

"I'm sorry to hear that," The Creator offered sympathetically. "Why do you think things are this way?"

"That's what I'm trying to figure out. U told me to be sure to encourage them often and I do so every chance I get," answered Z. "When I took this job, I was told only the most talented and energetic folks in all of Letterville would be on this project, but everywhere I look I see only lazy unproductive workers."

"Well, Z, I happen to know all of these workers and I can assure you that they are some of the finest workers in all the land," The Creator said as He surveyed the worksite. "Look closer and I think you'll see something else is going on."

"I'm not sure I understand," said Z.

"Well for starters, look at W. He is one of the finest woodworkers around, yet he hasn't touched a piece of wood since he started."

Instead, W was mixing concrete, which he found uncreative and extraordinarily boring. The best ironworker in all the land was I, yet he hadn't welded a single beam since he arrived. Instead, he was hammering, which he found repetitive and extraordinarily boring. D was an exceptional designer yet he wasn't designing. E loved electrical work but wasn't pulling wire. And though A was by far the best architect, he hadn't drawn a single line.

Everywhere they looked, they saw people doing exactly what they shouldn't. So, with Z's permission, The Creator sounded the whistle and called a meeting.

"F, do you like your job?" The Creator asked. "It's OK, be honest."

"No sir, not at all," F answered hesitantly.

"What do you love more than anything?"

"I love driving the forklift!" answered an eager F.

"Then that is what you shall do!" proclaimed The Creator.

And before you know it, supplies were being organized like never before.

"S, what about you?"

"I love to survey. It's what I was born to do!" answered S.

"Then go be the best surveyor you can be!"

And in a flash, S was marking the land like no one before.

"W, there's a stack of wood over there just waiting for your touch. Go be the best woodworker Letterville has ever seen!"

And he was.

The Creator continued, "Hello, I. Do you see those beams up there? How about you grab your welder's helmet and start climbing. I'm sure they could benefit from your expertise!"

And they did.

And so it continued until everyone was doing that which they love. And it showed.

A week later, The Creator stopped by again to check on the new center.

"Hello, Z."

A proud Z jumped up and said, "I was hoping you'd stop by. I haven't seen you in days."

"Indeed. But from the progress I see around here, it looks more like it's been a month!"

"We're two weeks ahead of schedule. Hard to believe, huh?" said Z.

"It's actually very easy to believe," answered The Creator, "that's what zeal will do for you!"

"Who is Zeal?" asked a confused Z. "I don't remember anyone around here by that name."

The Creator laughed and said, "It's not a who, it's a what. Zeal is what gets someone's heart beating."

"But what does that have to do with construction?" Z asked.

"It has everything to do with everything," said The Creator. "You see, Z, everyone has been made for something special: something for which they are passionate. And when that gets ignored, things don't always go as one would want. But when one listens to their heart's desire…"

"You get two weeks ahead of schedule!" Z interrupted.

The Creator chuckled and said, "I suppose that's one way to look at it!"

"Speaking of being ahead of schedule," Z said, "I am giving everyone tomorrow off so we can all attend the big party."

And for once The Creator did not smile His biggest smile for He knew what tomorrow had in store.

EPILOGUE

Not the End

The sun had risen and the sun had set many times since the day the letters were first presented to the citizens of Letterville. The rooster had crowed 365 times to be exact: for today was the anniversary of that magical day! All the fine people of Letterville know that special occasions merit a celebration of some sort, but an occasion as special as this deserved a party fit for a King – or in this case, The Creator!

A Great Banquet was planned and The Creator made sure every citizen of Letterville was invited for He had a very important announcement to make. So, unlike regular parties where folks seem to let things of non-importance get in the way of attending, great effort was made to make sure that everyone would attend. A handle all of the advertising. C made sure that it was marked on every calendar and helped everyone count down to the day. P made sure everyone was planning on attending and W spread the word that every shop and café would be closed - for work would not be permitted on this most special of days. And it was finally here!

"Ladies and Gentlemen! It is my honor to introduce, The Creator!" shouted the Master of Ceremonies as all the people rose to their feet and cheered. The people of Letterville loved The Creator more than anyone because of all the wonderful things He had done for them and this night they made sure He knew!

The Creator made His way to a magnificent table on which was spread an equally magnificent feast and then motioned for the procession of letters to begin.

"Ladies and Gentlemen! Please make welcome the letter A!" said the Master of Ceremonies.

The townspeople knew the Letters very well, for not only had the Letters taught them many great words but they had also helped them learn about Him…The Creator.

And so the crowd burst into applause as A entered the Great Hall. The Letters were to be seated in order, so A was escorted to his seat right next to The Creator who of course was seated at the head of the table. One by one, and in perfect order, the Letters continued to be presented and taken to their seats. That is until it was L's turn to enter. But as K was being lead into the room, and L was readying to enter, the Master of Ceremonies shouted, "Ladies and Gentlemen! The Letter…M."

The townspeople began whispering and wondering how a mistake such as this could happen – especially on a night like this! Everyone's eyes were fixed on The Creator for He knew the order of the letters better than anyone. But He sat silently and motioned for M to proceed.

L thought to himself, "Surely, they will realize this mistake and I will be next." as M entered the room. But the Master of Ceremonies then called for N and continued announcing letter after letter until even Z was at the table. Again, the room was filled with mumbling and confusion until The Creator raised His hand and immediately the room grew very, very quiet.

A drum roll thundered throughout the Great Hall and the Master of Ceremonies shouted in his most commanding voice of the night, "Ladies and Gentlemen! I present to you this evening's most honored guest. The Letter L."

Not sure he had heard correctly, L stood frozen in the doorway for a moment wondering what to do. The first few steps were quite a blur to L, but as he was escorted into the room he could smell the feast of all feasts, he could hear the triumphant music of the band and the thunderous applause of the townspeople, and at last he could see all the other Letters surrounding one very big table – with one very big problem. There was nowhere for him to sit! Around the longest table L had ever seen, were the Letters, seated in order, from A to Z. And right where his seat should be were K and M seated next to each other with no space between. Not even a little.

As L reached the table the band ceased playing and the crowd stopped applauding. The Creator rose to His feet, motioned for L to come near and said, "L, I want you to sit here at the head of the table."

Now completely bewildered, L stood motionless as he humbly said, "With all respect, sir, that is your seat. Maybe I should just make room here between K and M where I belong."

The Creator nodded and said, "This used to be my seat. But now it is yours."

"My seat?" L softly asked with confusion in his eyes, "I don't understand."

"Then let me explain", said The Creator in the kindest voice one has ever heard. "Around this table tonight are some of my greatest creations. And because of these letters, people far and wide have learned of me, and the plans I have for them.

The Creator lovingly looked at His creations and said, "G, you have helped people learn what it is to be good and giving. T, you have inspired people to try all kinds of great things. C, you have shown the meaning of compassion. The world is a kinder place thanks to you, K. P, people have more patience because of you. And J, you have brought much joy to my people."

Then as He looked around the table He said, "F and H, you have taught my people two of the greatest words of all: faith and hope. But there is a greater word; the greatest word this world has ever known. It is closer to my heart and describes me better than any word that has ever been spoken. And that word is love."

The Creator paused for a moment before continuing, "My friends, I must go away for a while and while I'm gone I need for all people to learn of me. So, L, I need you to sit here in my seat while I am away because only love has the power to show everyone what I am like. For I am Love."

As L took his place, the band began to play another song of celebration, and once again, everyone shouted and clapped for The Creator whom they were going to miss very much. As the feast began, laughter filled the air and conversation flowed as it does between the best of friends. Then after one last long look at His creation, The Creator slipped quietly out of the room, smiled His biggest smile, and said to Himself, "It is good. It is good..."

"...but it is not the end."

My Sincerest Thanks

First of all, through prayer and conversation, I have thanked God more times than I can remember for always showing up with ideas and inspiration. I want to thank Him again. Letterville is His.

If I'm honest, I've been dreading writing this part of the book since the day God planted the seed of Letterville within me, because I am fairly certain that with time the list of people I have innocently omitted will become larger than the one below. Still, rather than offer a generic note of gratitude, I will attempt to list some people who have supported me through my efforts to reflect The Creator.

Special thanks to Regina Jenkins. Because, it's a known fact that peacocks are bad at grammar.

Thank you to Kyle Watson, Frank Highland, Brian Holaway, Jeff, Carolee, Tori, Madeline, and Lily McPherson, Rob Touchstone, Beth Stubblefield, Terri Wheeler, Steve Cummings, Cody Doores, Mary Gill, Joy Hooper, Melanie Moon, Aly White, Rick Hatcher, Dave Clayton, Dave Culbreath, Jeff & Ruth Fox, Ron Charpentier, Charles & Emily Yingling, Todd Wigginton, Chris, Nicki, Madison, and Braden Soper, The Well Coffeehouse, Greg Petree, Wes Yoder, Norris & Ann Vickery, Jody Vickery, Rhonda & Kelvin Pennington, Daddy & Mama, and Adam & Taylor.

The above people are in no particular order, but I chose to save the best for last. Thank you to my wife, Laurie. You are simultaneously my rock and my pillow.

About the Author

Aaron is the co-founder and president of Punctum Media. Founded in 2010, Punctum Media is a non-profit organization that delivers creative content and encouragement to Jesus followers to aid in their efforts of spreading the Gospel.

Additionally, for 20 plus years he has been a songwriter, producer, and owner of 367 Music Publishing, and a staff writer for Music Genesis, Disney Music Publishing, Cal IV Music, and Curb Music.

I am amazed by creativity. It is humbling to me that the one true Creator shares inspiration with us and allows us the opportunity to in turn share that with others. I pray that you see Him in everything in which I am lucky enough to play a part.

Aaron

TWITTER
@aaronsain

INSTAGRAM
amsain

FACEBOOK
aaronsain

WEB
welcometoletterville.com
punctumedia.org

PUNCTUMEDIA
punctumedia.org

CPSIA information can be obtained
at www.ICGtesting.com
Printed in the USA
LVHW11s1151111018
593105LV00001B/262/P

9 780692 285046